# FRIED FEATHERS
# FOR THANKSGIVING

## by James Stevenson

 Greenwillow Books, New York

Library of Congress Cataloging-in-Publication Data
Stevenson, James, (date)    Fried feathers for Thanksgiving.
Summary: Mean witches Dolores and Lavinia try to spoil Thanksgiving
for everyone else but nice witch Emma and her friends outwit them.
[1. Witches—Fiction.   2. Thanksgiving—Fiction] I. Title.
PZ7.S84748Fr 1986    [E]    86-3100
ISBN 0-688-06675-5    ISBN 0-688-06676-3 (lib. ed.)